The
MISSING Bully

AN INTERACTIVE MYSTERY ADVENTURE

by Steve Brezenoff
illustrated by Marcos Calo

A Field Trip Mysteries Adventure
are published by Stone Arch Books
a Capstone Imprint
1710 Roe Crest Drive
North Mankato, Minnesota 55603
www.mycapstone.com

Library of Congress Cataloging-in-Publication Data

Names: Brezenoff, Steven, author. | Calo, Marcos, illustrator.
  Brezenoff, Steven. Field trip mysteries.
Title: The missing bully : an interactive mystery adventure / by Steve
  Brezenoff; illustrated by Marcos Calo.
Other titles: You choose books.
Description: North Mankato, Minnesota : Capstone Press, [2017] |
Series: Field trip mysteries | Series: You choose stories | Summary:
  When the class bully disappears on a field trip to the River City
  Zoo, James Shoo, known as "Gum," and the other sixth-grade detectives
  are determined to find out what happened, and it is up to the reader
  to choose what direction their investigation will take.
Identifiers: LCCN 2016027061 | ISBN 9781496526427 (library binding) |
  ISBN 9781496526465 (pbk.) | ISBN 9781496526502 (ebook) (pdf))
Subjects: LCSH: School field trips—Juvenile fiction. | Missing
  children—Juvenile fiction. | Zoos—Juvenile fiction. | Detective
  and mystery stories. | Plot-your-own stories. | CYAC: Mystery and
  detective stories. | Plot-your-own stories. | School field trips—
  Fiction. | Missing children—Fiction. | Zoos—Fiction. | GSAFD: Mystery
  fiction. | LCGFT: Detective and mystery fiction.
Classification: LCC PZ7.B7576 Mi 2017 | DDC 813.6 [Fic]—dc23 LC record
  available at https://lccn.loc.gov/2016027061

Graphic Designer: Kristi Carlson
Editor: Megan Atwood
Production Artist: Laura Manthe

Summary: When notorious bully Anton Gutman disappears during a field
trip to the River City Zoo, junior detectives Sam, Egg, Gum and Cat are
on the case!

Printed in Canada.
010050S17

YOU CHOOSE STORIES
A FIELD TRIP MYSTERIES ADVENTURE

The MISSING Bully

STONE ARCH BOOKS
a capstone imprint

Catalina Duran

A.K.A.: Cat

BIRTHDAY: February 15th

LEVEL: 6th Grade

INTERESTS:

Animals, being "green,"

field trips

Edward G. Garrison

A.K.A.: Egg

BIRTHDAY: May 14th

LEVEL: 6th Grade

INTERESTS:

Photography, field trips

James Shoo

A.K.A.: Gum

BIRTHDAY: November 19th

LEVEL: 6th Grade

INTERESTS:

Gum-chewing, field trips, and showing everyone what a crook Anton Gutman is

Samantha Archer

A.K.A.: Sam

BIRTHDAY: August 20th

LEVEL: 6th Grade

INTERESTS:

Old movies, field trips

FIELD TRIP 🚌 MYSTERIES

Mr. Spade's sixth-grade class is on a field trip at the River City Zoo.

At lunch, James Shoo — Gum, to his friends — says, "I'm beat."

"We still have a lot more walking to do after lunch, Gum," Catalina Duran says.

Samantha Archer sits directly across from them at the table and stares blankly.

"Earth to Sam," says Edward Garrison — known to his friends as Egg — sitting beside her.

Sam blinks. "Sorry," she says. "I've just been thinking how boring this field trip is."

"Boring?" Cat says. "Bird Land was like walking through a dream world!"

Sam shrugs. "It was fine," she says. "It's just not what I look for in a field trip."

TURN THE PAGE.

Gum takes a bite of his sandwich. "She means a mystery," he says. "Sam's only happy if we're solving a crime."

"How's this for a mystery?" Egg says, nodding to the far side of the cafeteria. "Check out Anton."

Anton Gutman — mean-spirited menace and all-around enemy of Sam, Egg, Cat, and Gum — sits alone at a table in the corner. Laid out in front of him are three textbooks, one notebook, a calculator, and two pencils.

Gum, twisting in his chair to see, says, "What's he up to?"

Cat, after glancing back at Anton, shakes her head. "He's studying," she says. "Don't stare."

"Anton," Sam says, looking at Cat with wide eyes, "is sitting *by himself* and *studying*. This doesn't seem odd to you?"

"It seems odd," Cat agrees. "But it's not a crime."

A whistle breaks through the din. Everyone quiets down and looks up. Mr. Spade stands in the center of the cafeteria.

"Everyone finish eating!" he says. "We've got one hour until the movie. Let's not waste it here."

The River City Zoo is hosting an exhibit of animatronic megafauna. The giant prehistoric mammals are also the focus of the movie the class will see as part of the field trip.

"Hurry, Gum," Egg says. He's already finished his lunch. He holds up his camera. "I'm itching to get some cool photos from the megafauna exhibit."

Gum crumples his empty foil and shoves it into the paper bag. "All right, I'm done. Two sandwiches, juice, milk, and a pudding cup sure hit the spot." He pops some gum into his mouth, as usual.

Cat smiles as she pushes her chair back. "Let's line up quickly so we have time. It's a long walk over there."

The four friends hurry to line up with the rest of their class. Mr. Spade walks the length of the line, counting kids as he goes.

TURN THE PAGE.

The two parent chaperones — Gloria Wendice's dad and Hiram Halliday's mom — stay at the front of the line.

"Fifteen, sixteen . . . ," Mr. Spade counts out loud.

Soon he reaches the back of the line and calls out, "Twenty-six." Then he says quietly, "Uh-oh."

Cat whispers, "There are twenty-seven of us in Mr. Spade's class. Someone's missing."

Sam grins and cracks her knuckles as Mr. Spade starts the count one more time.

"Stop it," Egg whispers at her.

"Stop what?" Sam asks, still grinning.

"You're excited that someone's missing," Egg says. "You've seen too many old movies with your grandpa."

"I am not excited!" she says. "Fine, maybe a little. But whoever it is, we'll find them, right?"

"Look at that," Cat says, pointing clear across the huge cafeteria. "Anton's lunch stuff. It's all still on the table."

"His books are gone, though," Gum points out.

Cat leaves the line to check it out. Sam, sensing a crime scene, hurries after her.

"Anything?" Sam asks as she walks up beside Cat.

Cat grabs a pencil from the floor. "How about this?"

"Get back in line, girls!" Mr. Spade says.

"Sorry, Mr. Spade," Sam says.

"You two, go with Ms. Halliday's group," Mr. Spade says to Cat and Egg. He looks at Sam and Gum. "And you two, you're with Mr. Wendice's group." To himself, he says, "I should call security, just to be safe."

Sam steps up to Mr. Spade. "Anton's missing, isn't he?" she asks.

Mr. Spade looks down at her and says, "He probably just stepped away without telling anyone. But, yes, Samantha. Anton is gone."

To follow Sam and Gum, turn to page 12.

To follow Cat and Egg, turn to page 14.

To see all four of them try to convince Mr. Spade to let them stay together, turn to page 16.

Sam, Gum, Cat, and Egg don't like separating on field trips, but sometimes the situation calls for splitting up. "We'll cover more of the zoo in two teams anyway," Sam says as the two groups leave the cafeteria.

"I don't like it," Cat says.

Egg takes her hand and pulls her gently along with Ms. Halliday's group. "We'll be fine," he says, and the groups head off in opposite directions.

Gum and Sam, with Mr. Wendice and his group, head to the Primate Forest. The wide, paved path grows narrow as they enter the cool, shaded woods.

Before long, they hear the howls of gibbons, the roars and barks of lowland gorillas, and the screams and hoots of chimpanzees.

"It's really like being in the wild," Mr. Wendice says, smiling. His daughter, Gloria, isn't smiling. She holds tightly to her dad's hand.

Gum senses she's frightened. "Hey, Gloria, how do monkeys get down the stairs?" After a beat, he says, "They slide down the banana-ster! Get it?" He chuckles at his own joke.

Gloria doesn't laugh.

The group rounds the first curve and reaches a fork in the path. A sign says **GORILLAS** to the right, and **ORANGUTANS** to the left. Mr. Wendice stops the group at the fork with his back to the nearby enclosure. Gloria stands next to him.

"Which way should we go, kids?" he asks.

But before the group can make a choice, a huge baboon in the enclosure behind Gloria and her father slams against the glass, letting loose a deafening screech.

Gloria, eyes wide in fright, takes off at top speed back the way the group came, screaming.

"Oh, no," says Mr. Wendice. "Gloria, wait!" He runs after her, leaving Sam and Gum standing alone at the fork in the path.

TO CHASE AFTER THEM, TURN TO PAGE 18.
TO STAY IN THE FOREST AND LOOK FOR CLUES, TURN TO PAGE 25.

"We'll be fine," Egg says to Cat, knowing she'd rather stay with Gum and Sam. "Besides," he adds as they follow behind Ms. Halliday and her son, Hiram, "we're heading to the Insect House. They have a butterfly garden."

Cat shrugs one shoulder. "Yeah," she admits. "That sounds pretty good."

"It's pretty crazy about Anton, huh?" Egg says.

Hiram overhears him and drops back. "You mean that he's missing? He probably just snuck off to cause trouble."

Egg had thought of that too. Still: "What if he didn't, though? What if he's in trouble?" he says.

Hiram's eyes narrow. "Then, good. He's always picking on me. I hope I never see him again."

With that, he catches up with his mom at the Insect House entrance.

"Which way is the butterfly garden?" Cat asks when Egg steps into the shade of the building.

Egg checks the map. "It's at the far end," he says. "Let's go."

Cat and Egg spend all their remaining time in the butterfly garden. It's outside, so the light is great for Egg's photos. Cat loves the smells of the flowers and the colors of the butterflies.

"Take a photo of me!" she says, and Egg snaps a bunch of pictures.

He notices the time on the display of his camera.

"We'd better get back to Ms. Halliday," he says. "Movie starts soon."

Egg and Cat run back through the Insect House.

"There you are," says Ms. Halliday, standing near the exit. "Time to go to the movie." She steps outside with the class.

Cat and Egg start to follow, but Cat grabs Egg's wrist. "Wait," she says. "Look at that."

A gray backpack leans against the outside wall of the Insect House building. Egg picks it up, checks the tag, and says, "It's Anton's."

To hurry to the movie and give the bag to Mr. Spade, turn to page 21.

To take the bag to the movie and rummage through it for clues, turn to page 27.

"Mr. Spade," Egg says, "would it be OK if Cat and I joined Gloria's dad's group?"

"What?" Mr. Spade says, distracted. "Sure. Whatever." He takes out his phone and starts to dial.

Mr. Wendice says, "Well, group, should we go to the megafauna exhibit?" The students all nod.

When they get to the woods where the exhibit is, mist from fog machines and sounds of a prehistoric forest drift toward them from speakers.

A robotic saber-toothed cat prowls in the undergrowth. As they pass, it snarls and swipes its huge paw.

The kids all jump, but Gloria especially. "I'm not going one step farther," she says, and walks back to the entrance to sit on a bench. Mr. Wendice, though, has already stomped ahead on the path.

Egg, too, doesn't notice Gloria's retreat. He's snapping photos of squawking birds.

Gum and Cat are distracted by the *Megatherium* — the giant sloth — so Sam moves to comfort Gloria.

Sam sits beside her on the bench, unsure of what to say. "So, um, your dad seems . . . nice."

"He's grumpy about Anton," Gloria says.

"Does he think Anton is in trouble?" Sam asks.

"Oh, no," Gloria says. "But Dad is the coach of the math team, and if Anton isn't back soon —"

"Wait," Sam says. "Anton is on the math team?"

Gloria nods. "Yup. And if he gets in trouble for running off, he'll miss the meet. The team will have to forfeit."

Cat jogs up to the bench. "You have to come see the baby *Deinotherium*," she says. "They're so cute."

"Cat," Sam says, "did you know Anton is on the math team?"

"I didn't know there was a math team," Cat says.

"Let's grab Egg and Gum," Sam says, rising from the bench. "This might be important."

TO TALK TO GLORIA'S DAD ABOUT THE MATH TEAM AND ANTON, TURN TO PAGE 23.
TO SUGGEST THE GROUP MOVE ON TO BIRD LAND, TURN TO PAGE 29.

Sam and Gum sprint through the darkness of the forest. The sounds around them grow louder, as if the monkeys and apes are watching them.

Ahead they see sunlight beyond the trees.

But the moment they exit the forest, they run smack into a huge man in a zoo uniform.

"Hold it," he snarls at them. He drops heavy hands on their shoulders. "No running allowed."

"We're just in a hurry," Gum says, trying to pull out of the man's grip.

"Yeah," Sam says. "Get your filthy meat hook off me, you big galoot."

The man's face turns red and his grip on their shoulders gets tighter.

"You're coming with me," he says.

The guard marches them all the way to the movie theater, where Mr. Spade and his group have just arrived.

"I assume these two troublemakers belong to you," he says, finally letting go of Sam and Gum.

Mr. Spade looks at the sleuths and says sternly, "Get to the movie." He turns to the security guard. "It might be time to call the police," Sam and Gum overhear him say.

They share a look. But they can't do much: they've hit a dead end. Sam shrugs.

"I'm going to the bathroom," she says. "Grab our seats." On the way to the bathroom, Sam spots Hiram's mom on the phone.

"I'll do whatever it takes," Ms. Halliday says into the phone.

Sam stops and eavesdrops.

Ms. Halliday continues, "As long as it keeps the Gutmans off our backs!"

A chill runs up Sam's spine. She hurries to the theater and tells Gum, Egg, and Cat what she overheard.

"What's our next step?" Gum asks.

To follow Hiram's mother to learn more, turn to page 32.
To question Hiram about the overheard conversation, turn to page 49.

Cat and Egg race through the zoo. Anton's book bag bounces in Egg's hand as he runs.

They zoom past Hiram and his mom. They arrive at the theater out of breath and find Mr. Spade waiting in front. Some kids from their class are already there, including Sam and Gum.

"Mr. Spade!" Cat says between gasps for breath. "We found Anton's bag!"

"Near the Insect House," Egg adds, handing the bag to their teacher.

"Well done," Mr. Spade says. "Thank you for bringing it to me. You did the right thing. Maybe we'll have some good news for his parents when they get here."

Sam is impressed too. She gives Egg a gentle punch in the arm, smiling.

"Well, in you go," Mr. Spade says. "It's almost movie time."

"Mr. Spade," Egg says, "aren't you going to open the bag? It might have a clue inside."

TURN THE PAGE.

"Of course not," Mr. Spade says. "I'll hand it over to zoo security. If there is a clue, they'll know what to do with it."

With that, he walks off.

"Now what do we do?" Egg says. "That was our only clue."

Cat nods over Egg's shoulder. "Maybe we should talk to them," she says.

Egg turns, and there, standing close together and cackling like hyenas, are Anton's two friends, Hans and Luca. Both of them are Sam's height and twice as wide.

"Only if Sam goes first," Egg says. Gum and Cat nod. None of them are brave enough to approach Anton's henchmen on their own, but behind Sam they can manage.

But Sam has other ideas.

"No way," Sam says. "That bag is the best lead we have, and we have to get it back."

To question the henchmen, turn to page 34.
To try to get the bag back, turn to page 53.

"Hey, Mr. Wendice," Sam says as she and her three best friends walk up to Gloria's dad. He's nearly done in the megafauna exhibit, and he has circled back toward the entrance.

"Yeah?" he says, just as grumpy as Gloria said he was. "Hey, where's Gloria?"

"Oh, she was a little scared," Sam says. "She's waiting for you at the exit."

Mr. Wendice grimaces. "Yeah, she scares a little easily sometimes," he says. "I'd better go find her."

"Just a second," Gum says. "Can we ask you something?"

"We hear Anton's on the math team," Egg says. "Is that true?"

Gum laughs. "I didn't even know he could count to ten!" he says.

Mr. Wendice shoots Gum a confused glare. "Sure, Anton's a mathlete," he says. "In fact, he's one of our best. Unfortunately, he's also a troublemaker, a wise guy, and a smart aleck. And I'm guessing he just ran off."

TURN THE PAGE.

"He is *definitely* a troublemaker," Gum says quietly.

"And if he gets detention," Mr. Wendice goes on, "we'll have to forfeit today's meet."

"So you'd lose?" Cat says.

Mr. Wendice nods. "Against North Middle School, our biggest rivals," he says.

"You're not even a little worried that he's gone?" Egg asks.

"Nope. This is just like him," Mr. Wendice says. "He isn't exactly reliable. I knew he was nervous, but this is ridiculous."

"Daddy!" Gloria calls from the bench. "It's time to go to the movie."

"Coming, snookums!" Mr. Wendice says, jogging toward his daughter.

"So what do you think?" Cat asks Egg, Gum, and Sam. "Is Anton hiding because he's nervous about the meet, or do you think it's something else completely?"

IF ANTON IS HIDING SO HE WON'T HAVE TO COMPETE IN THE MEET, TURN TO PAGE 37.

IF THE MATH MEET HAS NOTHING TO DO WITH THE MYSTERY, TURN TO PAGE 56.

When Mr. Wendice is out of sight, Gum and Sam begin wandering along the path, scanning for clues as they go.

"What should I be looking for?" Gum asks.

"Anything out of the ordinary," she says. "Scraps of paper, scuffed footprints, snapped branches, bloody fingerprints . . ."

"Whoa," Gum says. "If I find any bloody fingerprints, I'm calling the cops."

"Yeah, that would probably be a good idea," Sam says, and then she grabs Gum's wrist. "Shhh. You hear something?"

Gum listens, but he hears nothing.

Sam presses a finger to her lips. Then she crouches a little farther along the path. She stays hidden beside a huge fern, and Gum crouches beside her.

"Listen," Sam whispers.

Sure enough, Gum hears it too: a man's voice.

"Yeah, it's done," he says.

TURN THE PAGE.

No one replies, and a moment later he continues. "All taken care of, boss. He won't be going anywhere else today till we say so."

Sam and Gum strain to hear anything else, but the voice is silent. Soon, they hear footsteps and the *swish swoosh* of a broom.

"Hide!" Sam whispers at Gum. The two friends scurry along until they find a stone bench. Quickly, they duck behind it and watch the man pass.

He's a big guy, and he pushes a broom in front of him. He's wearing a zoo uniform.

Sam and Gum run the whole way back to the theater. Gloria and her father are already there, and so are Egg and Cat.

"We know who snatched Anton," Sam whispers to their two friends. She tells them what they overheard.

"I don't know," Cat says. "He could have been talking about anything. Let's just get inside and watch the movie."

TO GO TELL MR. SPADE THAT ANTON WAS KIDNAPPED BY THE ZOO EMPLOYEE, TURN TO PAGE 69.

TO WATCH THE MOVIE, TURN TO PAGE 87.

By the time Cat and Egg reach the theater, they're both out of breath. "I don't think I've ever run that fast!" Cat says, collapsing onto a bench in the movie theater's lobby.

"Can't rest now," Egg says, leaning on the arm of the bench, Anton's book bag dangling from his hand. "Gotta find Sam and Gum . . ."

"You rang?" Gum says as he and Sam sit on the bench next to Cat.

Egg holds out the bag. "We found this," he says. "It's Anton's."

Sam's mouth drops open as she jumps to her feet and grabs the bag. "Have you looked inside?" she asks.

"Not yet," Cat says. "We figured you'd want the first look, Detective."

Sam smiles and unzips the bag. The first thing she pulls out is a math textbook.

"Whoa," Egg says, taking the book from Sam and flipping through the pages. "This is way above sixth grade."

TURN THE PAGE.

"Is this what Anton was studying during lunch?" Cat wonders aloud.

Gloria is walking by, and she stops at Cat's question. "It probably is," she says. "He has a meet today."

"What kind of meat?" Gum says. "Roast beef? Prime rib? A nice rack of lamb, perhaps?"

"No, a meet," Gloria says. "Like, a competition. Anton is on the math team. So is Naomi." Gloria nods toward a girl at the concession counter, also from Mr. Spade's class. "My dad's the coach." She narrows her eyes at them. "Hey, is that Anton's bag? Where did you get that?"

"Oh, we found it," Sam says, quickly zipping it back up. "Just about to give it to Mr. Spade."

Gloria walks on, still eyeing the four friends suspiciously.

"Movie time, everyone!" Mr. Spade calls from the theater doors. "Let's go!"

To talk to Gloria's dad about the math team, turn to page 72.
To talk to Naomi, who is also on the math team, turn to page 90.

"Oh, I'm glad we're going back to Bird Land," Cat says. "We didn't get enough time in there this morning."

"How much time do you need?" Gum says, giving Cat a gentle shove.

"Leave her alone," Egg says, smiling. He holds up his camera. "I was hoping to get more shots of the hornbills, anyway."

Cat nods, eyes wide. "Their colors are so amazing," she says.

"And," Sam whispers to her friends, "I think Anton was there this morning. We might stumble onto a clue."

"We won't have very long here, kids," Mr. Wendice says, looking at his watch as the group reaches Bird Land. "The movie is in fifteen minutes."

"I don't think we'll even need that much time," Gloria says, stopping at the doors to Bird Land. "Look."

Turn the page.

Sam, Egg, Cat, and Gum stand around her. Yellow tape blocks both glass doors. A sign hanging from the tape says

CLOSED TODAY FOR REPAIRS

"Well, that's odd," Mr. Wendice says. "They didn't tell me Bird Land would be closed today."

"Why is that odd?" Gloria says, shrugging. She almost looks relieved not to have to go inside. "Do they usually notify you about repairs, Dad?"

Mr. Wendice shakes his head. "No, Gloria," he says, "but they told me and the other chaperones that only one of the exhibits was closed. And that was the Big Cats Exhibit."

"And what's weirder," Sam says, "is my friends and I were inside Bird Land this morning already. There were no repairs going on."

Gloria takes a step back from the Bird Land doors. "OK," she says, obviously frightened. "*That* is odd."

TO SNEAK INTO BIRD LAND ALONE TO INVESTIGATE WHY IT'S CLOSED, TURN TO PAGE 74.

TO CONVINCE GLORIA'S DAD TO INVESTIGATE WITH THEM, TURN TO PAGE 93.

Sam leads her friends through the crowded lobby. "I saw her over by the bathroom," Sam says.

"Do we have time for this?" Cat whispers. "The movie starts any minute."

"There she is!" Egg hisses. Ms. Halliday is on the phone again just outside the theater doors.

"We can't hear a thing in here," Gum says. "And she's walking away!"

Hiram's mom moves away from the theater until she's just out of sight, hidden behind a parked van.

"Come on," Sam says. After a quick look around to make sure no chaperones are watching, she pushes through the glass door to follow Ms. Halliday.

Gum follows at once. Egg glances at Cat.

"I don't know . . . ," Cat says.

Egg takes her hand. "Come on, they need us," he says.

They join Sam and Gum crouched behind the cement footing of a streetlight.

"Look, if this isn't going to fix things," Ms. Halliday says into her phone, "then maybe we have to call it off."

Sam and Cat share a look.

"If I have to make other arrangements . . . ," Ms. Halliday barks. "Just get the Gutmans off my back, all right?" A moment later, she stomps back into the theater. She doesn't seem to notice the four junior detectives crouched nearby.

When she's out of sight, Sam stands up. "What does Ms. Halliday have to do with Anton's family?" she says.

Gum shrugs. "Doesn't matter," he says. "We heard plenty. She's responsible for Anton's disappearance."

"And if she's not, she sure seems to know who is!" Egg points out.

"Let's go tell Mr. Spade," Cat says. "I've got the creeps in a big way, and the sooner this is over, the better."

TURN TO PAGE 39.

"There they are," Gum says, nodding toward Hans and Luca.

The two bulky boys stand close together halfway down the hallway that leads to the emergency exit. Their backs are to them.

"What are they up to?" Egg says.

"They're always up to something," Sam says and begins to walk over to them.

Cat grabs her arm. Gum grabs her wrist. Egg grabs her other wrist.

"Um, guys?" Sam says. "It's kind of hard to walk over there with you three holding me like this."

"You're just going to walk right up to them?" Cat asks, her voice shaky.

"They'll turn you into paste!" Egg says.

"They'll knock you into next week!" Gum says.

Sam rolls her eyes. "Please," she says, tugging herself away from her friends' grips. "They're all bark and no bite. Watch this."

She strides across the lobby and right up to Hans and Luca. "Hey," she says, "what are you two doing?"

The two turn around, their faces hard and mean. When they see Sam and her friends, though, they relax. "Well," says Hans, "if it isn't Samuel and her *dork* patrol."

"Good one, Hans," Sam says, walking right up to him. "Now, how about you tell us what happened to Anton?"

"Why would we do that?" Hans says, and he moves a little closer to Sam, as if he might knock her over or something.

"Come on," Gum says, finally hurrying over to join Sam. Egg and Cat run over too — though they stay behind Sam.

"Because," Sam says, not backing down, "we're trying to find him."

"Ha, ha," says Luca. "The nerd *detectives* are gonna solve the mystery!" He and Hans laugh and laugh.

"Tell you what," Gum says. "You tell us what you know about Anton, and we won't tell Mr. Spade we just busted you writing your names in marker on the emergency exit door."

TURN THE PAGE.

The two bullies step to the side and look at the door where their names are written in black marker. "We didn't do that," Luca says.

"Just a coincidence that it says your names, then?" Cat says.

They look at each other until finally Hans says, "Fine. You wanna know what we know? Nothing, that's what."

"It's true," says Luca. "We hardly ever see Anton anymore."

For a moment, Hans and Luca almost seem sad about it.

Cat steps in closer. In a soothing voice, she says, "We *did* see Anton eating alone during lunch. It looked like he was studying."

"He's always studying," Luca says, "lately."

"Whatever," Hans says. "Let's get out of here. I'm done talking to these nerds."

He and Luca shove past Sam, Gum, Egg, and Cat and stride through the lobby. Hans bumps Cat as he passes, almost knocking her down.

TURN TO PAGE 43.

As Mr. Wendice leads his group to the movie theater, the four junior detectives hang back to talk over the case.

"You know what I think?" Gum says, reaching into his pocket for his pack of gum. He pulls out three fresh cubes and pops them into his mouth.

His friends have no choice but to wait while he softens the three pieces of gum. Finally, Sam can't take it anymore.

"What?" she snaps. "What do you think?"

Gum grins and chews a couple more times. "I think Anton is hiding," he says.

"From what?" Cat says.

Gum shakes his head. "From *who*?" he says, correcting her.

"Actually," Egg says, "from *whom*? But go on."

"From Mr. Wendice," Gum says. He grins and shrugs. "It's obvious, really."

"Oh, obvious, is it?" Sam says, crossing her arms. Samantha Archer is not a junior detective who likes to be shown up, even by her own best friends.

TURN THE PAGE.

Gum nods. "You heard him back there," Gum says. "He's worried Anton might get detention — not at all worried something's happened to him. I mean, would you want to have that guy as a coach? I might run away too."

"Gum has a point," Cat says. "I bet Mr. Wendice can be pretty tough when the mathletes make mistakes."

"Maybe the pressure got to him," Egg says.

"So," Sam says, "what do we do?"

"We find Anton," Gum says, and the four friends stop walking.

"Now?" Cat says. "But . . . we're supposed to go to the movie!"

Egg, Sam, and Gum exchange glances.

"Sorry, Cat," Sam says. "Three to one. You coming?"

With that, Egg, Sam, and Gum turn and jog back toward the zoo's main building. Cat waits a moment, sighs, and then hurries after them.

Turn to page 46.

"It's so crowded!" Egg says.

Sam spots Mr. Spade standing with a woman in a zoo security uniform. "There he is!" she says.

"Excuse us!" Gum shouts, shoving through the mass of students and zoo visitors.

"Make way!" Sam says beside him.

Together, they clear a path. By the time they reach Mr. Spade, most of the class has gathered around to see what the fuss is all about.

"Mr. Spade," Cat says, "we've been tracking down Anton."

Mr. Spade looks down his nose at her. "I exhibit no surprise, Ms. Duran," he says. "And you happened to catch me talking with the zoo's head of security. So what did you find out?"

Sam faces Mr. Spade. She's almost as tall as he is. "I overheard Ms. Halliday on the phone."

"And?" the security chief says.

Sam pulls her notebook from her back pocket and recites word-for-word what Ms. Halliday said.

TURN THE PAGE.

"I think the transcript speaks for itself," Sam says, putting away the notebook.

Egg steps up next to her and says to the two adults, "Yep. We think Ms. Halliday snatched Anton to get back at the Gutmans."

"For what?" the zoo security chief says.

"We don't know that part," Sam admits quietly.

Just then, Ms. Halliday shoves through the crowd.

"Ms. Halliday!" Gum says. "How long have you been there?"

"Long enough," she snaps. "I heard the whole thing, and I won't stand for it!"

The zoo's security chief steps up to Ms. Halliday.

"Ms. Halliday, maybe you can explain the phone call these kids say they heard," she says.

"You bet I can," she says, laughing. "Overactive imaginations! Sure, I made a couple of phone calls. But this nonsense about the Gutmans? Utter fantasy. I never said anything like that."

She turns to Sam, her expression a little *too* indignant. Sam doesn't buy it. "Besides," Ms. Halliday says, "what possible motive could I have to do anything to little Anton?"

Sam and her friends are stumped. They don't know what Ms. Halliday's motive could have been. None of them says a word.

The security chief clucks her tongue and sighs. "Well, I guess this was a waste of time," she says. "I'd better check in with my team and see what they've come up with."

"And you kids had better get inside," Mr. Spade says. "The movie is about to start."

"But what about Anton?" Cat says. "We still don't know where he is."

"The security team will find him soon, I'm sure," Mr. Spade says. "This is a good lesson for you and your friends. You can't go around accusing people of crimes without evidence!"

THE END

TO FOLLOW ANOTHER PATH, TURN TO PAGE 11.

"You four!" Mr. Spade's deep voice bellows across the lobby. "Why aren't you in the theater yet? The movie's about to start!"

Cat glances at her friends before running over to Mr. Spade. "We'll go in right away, Mr. Spade," she says. "But . . . well, it's about Anton."

"What about him?" Mr. Spade says. "Have you heard anything?"

"We've heard a *lot*," Cat says as Sam, Gum, and Egg join her.

"We have?" Gum asks under his breath.

"For starters," Cat goes on, undeterred, "we found his bag at the Insect House."

"Right," Mr. Spade says. "You gave me the bag, and I passed it on to the security team. What else?"

"And we just got done talking to Hans and Luca," Cat goes on. "They're Anton's best friends. And they said he's been studying all the time."

"All the time," Egg puts in. "They never see him anymore."

TURN THE PAGE.

"Right," Mr. Spade says. "He joined the math team. I noticed that."

"So we think," Cat goes on, "that probably Anton is hiding somewhere so he can *keep* studying even though we're supposed to be touring the zoo and watching a movie and stuff."

Mr. Spade looks at Cat for a long time. He glances at the others in turn, and then back at Cat. "That's an interesting theory, Catalina." He looks past the kids and waves at a woman in a zoo security uniform. She heads their way after speaking briefly into her walkie-talkie.

"Where do you think he might be hiding?" Mr. Spade asks Cat.

"Our best guess," Sam says, "is the Insect House, since that's where Cat and Egg found his bag."

"But weren't you there just a few minutes ago?" Mr. Spade asks as the security woman reaches them. "It's a long shot, but perhaps you can check it out, Ms. Hastings?"

Mr. Spade — with a few interruptions from Cat and her friends — explains the theory to Ms. Hastings, the zoo's chief of security. She nods seriously, talks into her walkie-talkie, and then waits.

The kids wait too. Mr. Spade waits. They can hear the opening theme of the megafauna movie starting in the theater behind them.

After a couple of minutes, Ms. Hastings' walkie-talkie crackles. She pulls it from her hip and steps away to answer.

"This will be our answer," Mr. Spade says, giving Cat's shoulder a squeeze. "I hope you kids are right about this."

But when Ms. Hastings returns, she shakes her head. "Nothing," she says. "Not a sign of the boy."

She turns to Cat, Sam, Egg, and Gum. "Don't you kids worry," she says. "We'll find your friend soon enough. It was a good idea."

"Now go watch the movie," Mr. Spade says.

THE END

TO FOLLOW ANOTHER PATH, TURN TO PAGE 11.

"You guys!" Cat yells from the back of the pack of four. "Where are we even *going*?"

"It's just a hunch," Sam says from the front, "but if I were Anton, I'd go to the one place no one is probably searching."

"The cafeteria," Gum adds, glancing over his shoulder at Cat, a grin playing on his lips.

"It would have been smart to double back," Egg adds. "Once Mr. Spade and the security team had a look around, they probably wouldn't look there again."

Cat nods as she jogs up to Egg. "Are we sure Anton would be smart enough for that?"

Sam shrugs. "Well, he's a mathlete and we didn't know it!"

The four pass the wooded entrance to the Primate Forest. From inside, they hear the screeching and howls of monkeys and apes.

They hurry past the tinted glass doors of the Insect House, gaining speed.

Bird Land is a blur as the four zip past. Out of the corner of her eye, Cat notices yellow tape across the doors. Bird Land is closed, though it was open this morning. It's odd, but she can't stop now. Gum and Sam are too far ahead.

Egg's camera bounces against his chest. He has to grab it with one hand to keep it steady.

"Hey, you kids!" shouts a man dressed in a green uniform. He's pushing a broom on one of the side paths. "No running! Get back to your group!"

But Egg doesn't stop. Up ahead, Sam and Gum don't stop either.

Egg grabs Cat's hand. He knows she'd like to stop. Cat follows the rules — most of the time.

The automatic doors slide open. Sam slips in sideways before they've finished opening and flies down the long hallway to the cafeteria — past the penguins behind glass, past the indoor Tropical Walk, and past the gift shop.

TURN THE PAGE.

She reaches the cafeteria and bursts in. The place is deserted.

The sleuths spend fifteen minutes looking, but they still can't find Anton.

"Um, guys?" Egg says. "Looks like Anton isn't our only problem right now."

Mr. Spade, Mr. Wendice, and three members of the zoo's security staff stride into the cafeteria together.

"That's the last straw!" Mr. Spade says. "You'll wait for your classmates on the bus with Mel."

"Oh, no. The bus driver, Smelly Melly?" Gum asks.

Mr. Spade and Mr. Wendice escort the four failed junior detectives onto the bus.

"Hey, guys," Mel says from the driver's seat as Gum, Sam, Egg, and Cat climb onto the bus. "I was just about to enjoy this delicious egg salad, onion, and pickle sandwich. Doesn't it smell terrific?"

THE END

TO FOLLOW ANOTHER PATH, TURN TO PAGE 11.

The four friends look for Hiram and find him sitting alone in the back of the theater. The movie hasn't started yet, and the house lights are still up.

"Cat," Egg says, putting a hand on her shoulder, "you should do the talking."

"Cat?" Sam stops. "Since when does Cat do the interrogations?"

Egg shrugs. "No offense, Sam," he says, "but Hiram is shy. You'd intimidate him."

Cat glances at Sam and Egg. Sam nods reluctantly, so Cat walks over to Hiram. "Anyone sitting here?" she asks.

Hiram shakes his head, and Cat sits down next to him.

"I hope there's a lot about the giant sloths in this movie," Cat says.

Hiram doesn't answer right away. He sniffs and shifts in his seat. "I like the woolly mammoths," he finally says.

Turn the page.

"Yeah, me too," Cat says. "I bet it'd be fun to ride one!"

Hiram smiles.

"So, I heard about what Anton Gutman's family is doing," Cat bluffs, fiddling with the zipper of her jacket. "Must be hard."

Hiram looks at her, his eyes wide. "You heard about that?"

Cat shrugs. "Sure," she says. "Everyone's heard, right? It doesn't seem fair."

She glances at Sam, Egg, and Gum, who stand in the aisle and nod encouragingly.

"No, it's not," Hiram says. "I mean, Mom's hardware store has been in that spot on Main Street for fifty years. Her dad opened it before she was even born."

"Right," Cat says, beginning to get it. She knows the old hardware store in downtown River City. She didn't know the Hallidays owned it, though.

"Now the Gutmans are opening their huge hardware store right across the street, practically," Hiram continues. "Mom's store doesn't have a chance of surviving."

Cat's eyes go wide as she looks at her friends in the aisle. Sam whips out her notebook and scribbles something down.

"Wow," Cat says as she gets to her feet. "That sounds awful."

"Wait, where are you going?" Hiram says. "The movie's about to start."

"Right, um . . . ," Cat says, backing into the aisle to join her friends, who have left the theater for the lobby. "I'll be back as soon as I can. Save my seat, OK? Thanks, Hiram!"

Cat dashes from the theater and meets Sam, Gum, and Egg in the lobby, where they are waiting for her.

"That's enough of a motive for me," Sam says, slapping the cover of her little notebook. "Let's go tell Mr. Spade. If my hunch is right, Ms. Halliday will know exactly where to find Anton."

TURN TO PAGE 59.

"I don't think this is a great idea," Cat says. She follows Sam, Gum, and Egg as they hurry behind Mr. Spade.

Their teacher holds Anton's book bag in one hand as he walks across the zoo's central concrete plaza. It's a cool day, so the giant sprinklers shaped like bears — a mama bear, papa bear, and baby bear — are off.

Today they work pretty well to hide behind, so their teacher doesn't see them tailing him.

"I don't like this," Cat hisses from behind the baby bear sprinkler.

Sam looks over from behind the mama bear sprinkler, where she's hiding with Egg. "Shhh!" Sam hisses back, her eyes narrowed.

Mr. Spade waits at the door of a squat red building. A narrow sign over the door reads

ZOO SECURITY OFFICE
OFFICIALS ONLY

After a moment, he opens the door and goes inside.

TURN THE PAGE.

Sam runs around the side of the building and takes position under a window. She looks back at her friends and waves them over.

"Are we really doing this?" Cat asks as Gum shuffles past.

Gum grins at her and nods. "Come on!"

Cat squeaks nervously through gritted teeth, but she shuffles along with him and Egg to crouch with Sam at the window.

Sam slowly rises to the window and peeks inside. "He's handing over the book bag," she narrates. "Some lady took it. She's setting it down next to her desk. Here they come!"

She drops down from the window and presses herself against the brick building. A moment later, Mr. Spade and the woman from zoo security come out of the building and walk together back toward the movie theater.

"Coast is clear," Gum says, standing up.

"Let's go," Sam says, and she hurries around to the front of the building.

"Wait a second," Cat says. "You can't just go in there! It says 'officials only.'"

"It doesn't say official what, though," Gum says. "I'm officially awesome, for example."

Sam tries the handle. "It's unlocked," she says. She opens the door slowly and sticks her head in. "I'm going in."

"Oh, no," Cat says, squatting just outside the door.

"It'll be all right," Egg says.

Cat holds her breath, but she's worried for nothing. Sam returns, Anton's bag in one hand.

"You did it!" Cat says. "Oh, Sam. You are crazy."

"Crazy like a fox," Sam says. She crouches down with the bag. "Now let's see what old Anton is hiding in here," Sam says.

But before she can even tug open the zipper, a whistle blows and security officers shout.

"Uh-oh," Sam says, looking up as her face goes pale. "Busted."

TURN TO PAGE 63.

"I'm telling you," Sam says. "We're barking up the wrong tree."

"What do you mean?" Cat says.

"Whatever's going on here," Sam says, "it has nothing to do with the math meet. It's a classic red herring."

Gum shakes his head. "Herring aren't red," he says. "They're silvery."

"Not once they've been cured and smoked," Sam says. "And they smell really strong — strong enough to pull a tracking dog off the trail."

"Or a detective off the case," Egg says.

Cat says, "Ohh. That's where that saying comes from."

Sam taps her nose. "This math meet," she says. "It's a distraction. My guess is Anton is mixed up in some bad stuff."

Mr. Wendice calls from the wooded entrance to the megafauna exhibit. "Time for the movie, kids!" he yells. "Get a move on."

"How can we look for clues while we're sitting in a dark movie theater?" Cat says. The four junior detectives slowly follow Mr. Wendice and Gloria.

"Time to make the big sacrifices, guys," Sam says. She stops just outside the megafauna exhibit and slips her hands into the pockets of her jeans.

Gum pulls out a piece of gum and pops it into his mouth.

Egg and Cat, two steps past their friends, stop and turn around to face them.

"Are you serious?" Cat says. "We're just going to *not go*?"

"We'll get in trouble," Egg points out.

Gum shrugs and drops onto a bench. "Nah," he says, chewing his gum. The scent of artificial flavor wafts from him. "Mr. Wendice is distracted by that silly math meet — the red herring."

"What if Mr. Spade does another head count before the movie starts?" Egg says.

Cat nods. "He totally will."

TURN THE PAGE.

"By then we'll have found a clue," Sam says.

"Heck, by then we'll have found *Anton*," Gum says. "We'll show up at the theater as heroes!"

It wouldn't be the first time Egg and Cat broke the rules for Sam and Gum's crazy ideas.

"All right," Cat says. She glances over her shoulder. Gloria and her dad are well out of sight. "Where to?"

"We'll start at the cafeteria," Sam says. She turns to face Egg. "We didn't check out the scene of the crime. You snap some photos. I'll take some notes."

"What about us?" Gum says, pointing to himself and Cat.

"Witnesses," Sam says. "Lots of people were in the zoo's cafeteria. Someone must have seen something. Do we have a photo of Anton to show people?"

"I probably have one in here somewhere." Egg pats the camera around his neck.

"Great," Sam says. "Let's go."

TURN TO PAGE 66.

They find Mr. Spade in the lobby. He's standing with a woman in a zoo security uniform.

"Excuse us, Mr. Spade?" Cat says, tapping her teacher on the arm. "We may have some news about Anton."

The woman from zoo security perks up. "You have some information about the missing boy?"

"Yes," Sam says, pulling out her notebook. "Listen to this."

When Sam's done, the zoo security woman asks, "And where is Ms. Halliday?"

Ms. Halliday appears from out of nowhere. "Did I hear my name?"

"Ms. Halliday," Mr. Spade says, "do you know where Anton Gutman is?"

"Me?" Ms. Halliday asks. "Why would I have any idea where that troublemaker has gotten to?"

"A troublemaker, just like his parents, huh?" Sam says.

"And their coming-soon hardware store," Cat adds.

TURN THE PAGE.

"Yeah," Gum says. "It'll sure mean a lot of trouble for any little hardware stores on Main Street already. Like yours, for instance."

Ms. Halliday turns to Mr. Spade and snaps, "Those miserable Gutmans would love to see my hardware store shuttered, with a big, nasty For Lease sign on the door."

"Ms. Halliday," Mr. Spade says, "I had no idea. What a shame!"

"Shame indeed," Ms. Halliday says. "But I have no intention of letting that happen. That's why we've decided to delay Anton until his parents agree to cancel their plans to open that monstrosity on Main Street!"

The security officer clicks on her walkie-talkie. "I've got the kidnapper here," she says.

"Kidnapper!" Ms. Halliday says, eyes wide and alarmed. "Isn't that kind of a strong word? We're just *delaying* him."

"Yes, I'll hold her till the police arrive to arrest her," the security officer continues into the walkie-talkie.

"Arrest?" Ms. Halliday says, alarmed. "Wait a minute. I'll tell you where Anton is. We only wanted the Gutmans to listen to us!"

"Where is he?" Mr. Spade says.

"He's in Bird Land," she says. "My husband is with him. We made it look like the building is under repair."

"You get all that?" the security officer says into the walkie-talkie. "Great. Go get him."

The security officer pulls handcuffs from her belt. "You're still under arrest," she says, taking Ms. Halliday by the wrist.

Mr. Spade turns to Cat, Egg, Sam, and Gum. "I must say, I'm impressed," he says.

"Cat gets a lot of the credit," Sam says. "She knew just how to talk to our key witness."

Cat's eyes go wide. "I have to go!" she says, hurrying back to the theater. "Hiram is all alone in there!"

THE END

TO FOLLOW ANOTHER PATH, TURN TO PAGE 11.

In seconds, three zoo security officers surround the four junior detectives. One of them pulls out his walkie-talkie. It crackles to life.

"We've got the situation in hand, ma'am," he says.

Sam squints up at him. The sunlight reflects in his mirrored sunglasses. "Is there a problem, officers?" she asks.

"All right," he says. "On your feet."

The other two guards reach down and grab Sam by the arms as her friends stand up to protest.

"Officers, we can explain," Sam says.

She's smiling, though. It's obvious why to her friends. After all the old movies Sam's watched with her grandpa — stories of hard-boiled detectives on the wrong side of the law — she's getting a kick out of this.

But before she can launch into her explanation, Mr. Spade shouts from across the plaza. He and the security officer he gave the bag to earlier run toward them.

TURN THE PAGE.

"What happened here?" Mr. Spade asks, a little out of breath. No one has to answer, though. Mr. Spade figures it out pretty quickly.

He frowns and rubs his face, exasperated.

"Samantha," he says. His voice has that calmness grown-ups get when they've been mad and are now somewhere deeper than mad, way down in their minds. "Did you actually *break into* the security office and *steal* Anton's bag?"

"Like I said," Sam says, sticking out her chin, "we can explain."

Mr. Spade grabs Anton's bag and unzips it. "Did you expect to find some clue in here?" he says, pulling out a math textbook. "It's just Anton's books, Sam."

But Egg says, "That's some pretty advanced math. Why does he have that?"

Cat, Sam, Egg, and Gum look to Mr. Spade for the answer.

Mr. Spade, though, just shoves the book back into the bag. "I'm very disappointed in the four of you," he says. "And you'll spend the rest of our time at the zoo on the bus."

"But we'll miss the movie!" Cat protests. "I wanted to see the giant sloths!" She glares at Sam.

"Let that be a lesson to you," Mr. Spade says. "Apologize to these people and off you go."

"Nice going, Sam," Cat says, her chin wobbling.

Sam sticks out her chin even further. "I regret nothing!" But, looking at Cat's teary eyes weakens her resolve.

She puts her arm around Cat. "Maybe we can have our own field trip some other time?"

Cat smiles through her tears. "Yeah, OK. Except I'm guessing you'll find another mystery we'll have to solve."

Sam grins back. "Here's hoping!"

THE END

TO FOLLOW ANOTHER PATH, TURN TO PAGE 11.

A mom and her three kids sit at the table closest to the cafeteria doors. A couple more families sit here and there, digging into their paper bags and plastic lunch containers.

A dad and his little girl share a plate of chicken fingers and fries at the little round table in the back.

Two employees stand behind the counter at the grill, chatting.

The whole cafeteria hums with the tones of people talking. The four junior detectives take in everything.

"There's Anton's table," Cat says, crossing her arms. "His garbage is still there."

"Let's check it out," Sam says, glancing at Egg. The two head over to the table. Cat watches as Egg snaps photos and Sam examines the crumpled paper bag from every angle.

"Ready?" Gum says. "I'll try the two at the grill. You take the families, OK?"

"Sure," Cat says, squaring her shoulders.

But after fifteen minutes of photos and theories and chatting with moms and dads and little kids, they are no closer to solving this case.

"Now what?" Cat says, slumping into a booth near the cafeteria window. "We've found absolutely nothing."

Egg checks the time. "Maybe we should run over to the theater," he says. "We can slip in when it's dark. No one will notice."

Suddenly a man in a zoo uniform bursts into the cafeteria. He scans the room, and when his eyes fall on the four friends at the booth, he snarls and charges them.

"Whoa!" Gum says. "Who's this guy?"

Cat shakes her head. Egg snaps a photo.

"I don't know," Sam says, grabbing Cat's hand. "But he's here, he's after us, and there's already one kid missing."

"You think he's the kidnapper?" Cat says.

"I don't wanna find out the hard way," Sam says. "Run!"

TURN THE PAGE.

68

"The theater!" Gum says. "If he follows us, he'll run right into Mr. Spade!"

The four friends sprint across the plaza. Up ahead, Mr. Spade and a woman in a security uniform stand in front of the theater.

When they reach the adults, Gum says, "It's . . . ," but he can't catch his breath.

"Kidnapper!" Egg says.

"That man chased us across the plaza!" Sam says.

"Of course he did," the woman from security says. "That's Paul, our head of maintenance. Everyone's been looking for you."

"Looking for us?" Cat says. "Uh-oh."

"'Uh-oh' is right," Mr. Spade says. "One missing kid is enough for one day, but you made it five. You four will spend the rest of the field trip on the bus! Get moving!"

THE END

TO FOLLOW ANOTHER PATH, TURN TO PAGE 11.

"Why is it so crowded in here?" Sam says, leading her friends through the mob.

"Do you see Mr. Spade?" Egg asks. As one of the shortest kids in sixth grade, his view is blocked.

"Nope," Sam says. "But I do see the man we overheard in the Primate Forest. He's skulking," she says. "I've seen that look on a guilty man's face a thousand times."

"You have?" Gum says.

Egg shushes him. "She's getting into the zone," he says.

Gum nods. "Ah," he says.

"Let's shadow him," Sam says.

"Huh?" Cat says.

"Follow him," Sam explains quickly. "Let's *follow* him."

She shoves her way through classmates and strangers. Behind her, Gum snaps his gum, saying "excuse me" and "sorry" as he, Cat, and Egg follow.

Finally they reach the edge of the crowd.

TURN THE PAGE.

"There he is!" Sam announces.

Pushing a large gray plastic trash tub on wheels, the man in green vanishes into a darkened hallway.

"After him!" Sam shouts.

The others hurry after her. Egg and Cat can't keep up, and by the time they reach Sam, she's halfway down the dark hallway. Up ahead, a pair of heavy doors closes.

"Oh, no!" Cat says as the four friends hurry up to the double doors. A sign on one of them reads

EMPLOYEES ONLY

"What rotten luck," Gum says.

Sam kicks the wall. "Did you see that thing he was pushing? Big enough to carry a kid Anton's size, wouldn't you say?"

Cat's face goes pale as she sees the determination in Sam's expression. "Sam, you can't be serious. You can't mean . . ."

"We'll never know," Sam says, "unless we follow him in."

Turn to page 76.

"Mr. Wendice," Egg says, "can we talk to you?"

Egg, Cat, Sam, and Gum walk alongside their parent chaperone. Gloria walks farther ahead.

"Sure thing," Mr. Wendice says. "What's up?"

"You coach the math team, right?" Sam says.

Mr. Wendice looks surprised. "Most students at Franklin don't seem to know there *is* a math team."

"Oh," Gum says, laughing, "we didn't, but —"

Egg elbows him. "Of course they do," he says. "Everyone loves the math team."

Mr. Wendice smiles.

"And Anton is on the team," Cat adds. "Right?"

Mr. Wendice stops walking. The four junior detectives stop walking too. "Surely such big math team fans must *know* Anton Gutman is one of our star mathletes."

The four friends exchange a glance. "Oh, of *course*," Cat says. "We know that."

Mr. Wendice nods and walks on. Cat, Egg, Gum, and Sam hurry along with him.

Mr. Wendice continues, "Anton joined the team just two weeks ago. He has a gift for math."

"Wow," Cat says. "And there's a meet today?"

Mr. Wendice nods and checks his watch. "I sure hope Anton is OK," he says. "If he misses that meet — well, we'll lose for sure. And against North Middle School too."

Mr. Wendice begins walking faster. He waves and calls up to Gloria, "Wait up a minute, pumpkin! Don't get too far ahead!" With that, he takes off at a jog to catch his daughter.

"What do you think?" Sam says to her friends.

"Maybe it's all about the math meet," Egg says. "If Anton doesn't turn up, North wins."

"Right?" Cat says.

"So maybe someone from North is here at the zoo," Gum says, "and they wanted Anton out of the way."

TURN TO PAGE 80.

Mr. Wendice wraps his arms around his daughter and shuffles her away. Cat, Egg, and Sam follow, but Gum hangs back.

"We're not really going to just walk away from this, are we?" Gum says.

Sam glances at Egg and Cat. "What do you mean?" she asks.

Gum rolls his eyes. "It's so obvious!" he says. "Bird Land isn't closed. This is obviously a . . . a . . ."

"Ruse?" Sam suggests.

"That's it," Gum says. "A ruse. I bet Anton is in there."

"I don't know," Cat says. "It's taped off. We're not supposed to go in."

"Besides," Egg says, "Gloria and her dad are probably halfway to the movie theater by now. We should catch up."

Gum shakes his head. "No way," he says. "Bird Land is the key to this whole thing, and I'm going in. If you want to leave me here all alone, go right ahead."

"You all make me crazy sometimes," Cat says as Sam and Gum duck under the yellow tape.

Gum pushes the glass door. "It's open," he says. "Let's go."

"All right, all right," Cat says, taking Egg's hand and pulling him along. "Wait for us. We're coming too."

Bird Land is in a low, wide building and the open outdoor area beyond it is covered over with a net to keep the zoo birds in their enclosures.

As they enter, it takes a few moments for their eyes to adjust to the darkness of the entryway. Soon things take shape around them: statues of ancient and extinct birds, a long timeline of the Aves class of animals, and a curtain of bamboo hanging in a doorway.

"They keep it dark in here so the birds won't want to fly out," Cat says. "They stay in the light — they don't like the dark."

"I'm not loving the dark much right now myself," Gum admits.

TURN TO PAGE 83.

"It's probably . . . " Cat says, as Sam is about to bang the doors open.

They swing open, letting in a flood of bright light.

"Locked," Cat finishes.

Sam bolts through the doors into a huge warehouse. Sounds of people working echo through the cavernous space.

"Where'd he go?" Sam says.

"Sam," Egg says, "there is the possibility that the man in green was simply taking out the garbage."

"You two didn't hear him on the phone," Gum says. "He sounded so —"

"Sinister," Sam finishes for him.

Egg and Cat glance at each other and shrug.

"Come on," Sam says. She cautiously walks deeper into the warehouse.

All they find are people carrying huge sacks of food and cardboard boxes, or forklifts hauling unmarked wooden crates and piles of sod.

"He's not here," Egg says.

Just then, the forklift's beeping stops, along with its engine. For a moment, there is silence.

After a moment, the silence is broken by the uneven squeak of wheels.

"Hide!" Sam says. She grabs Cat by the hand and leads her friends around the corner, behind a stack of crates.

They hold their breath and listen as the wheels squeak closer and closer. When they nearly reach the kids' hiding place, though, a walkie-talkie crackles.

The squeak stops.

"Repeat, please," says a voice. The walkie-talkie crackles again. "Ah, roger that," the man says. "If I see those four kids, I'll grab them."

Cat gasps. Gum covers her mouth with his hand.

"Who's there?" the man snaps. "You'd better come out. I don't like being spied on!"

TURN THE PAGE.

"Run!" Sam shouts. Together, the kids dart out from their hiding place — right into the man in green.

He grins at them and says into the walkie-talkie, "I got 'em. Warehouse."

Mr. Spade, along with a couple of officers from zoo security, walk in. They must have been just outside the door. "Care to explain yourselves?" Mr. Spade says.

"I'm as confused as you are," Sam says. She tells Mr. Spade about the conversation she and Gum overheard earlier.

"You thought I was talking about the missing kid?" says the man in green, laughing. "Nah. I fixed the emu enclosure. Kept letting himself out."

"Oops," Sam says, her face going red.

"Looks like you four jumped to conclusions," Mr. Spade says. "I think you'll spend the rest of this field trip on the bus."

THE END

TO FOLLOW ANOTHER PATH, TURN TO PAGE 11.

The four walk to the theater. Cat reaches for the door.

"Just a second," Sam says, taking Cat's hand. She leads her, Egg, and Gum toward the edge of the sidewalk. "Look at that."

Her three friends stand beside her, looking toward the huge parking lot.

"Um," Gum says, "look at what?"

"Buses," Sam says. "Two rows of big, beautiful, yellow buses. If my guess is correct," she continues, pacing on the curb in front of her friends, like a lawyer in front of a jury, "one of those buses will be from North Middle School."

"Ooh," Cat and Egg say at the same time.

"But which one?" Gum says. "They all say things like Rivertown Bus Company. They don't say the name of the *school*."

Sam stops pacing. "We'll search them," she says.

"You're off your rocker," Gum says, eyes wide.

Cat nods. "Yeah," she says. "We should just get inside and watch the movie."

"And leave the crime unsolved?" Sam asks.

No one answers.

"Good," Sam says. "Now let's go."

She steps off the curb, and at the same instant, the group hears, "Just a minute, Samantha!"

"Mr. Spade!" Sam says, hopping back onto the curb.

Mr. Spade says, "The four of you, get inside the theater. One missing kid is enough today."

Gum, Egg, and Cat start for the theater doors. But Sam puts her fists on her hips and steps up to Mr. Spade.

"But that's why we're out here," Sam says. "To find the missing kid!"

"For the last time, Samantha," Mr. Spade says, "you're not a detective."

"Not *officially*," Sam says. "But did you know Anton is on the math team?"

TURN THE PAGE.

"Of course," Mr. Spade says.

"And did you know that without Anton, Franklin Middle School will lose the meet against North Middle School this afternoon?" Sam says.

"No," Mr. Spade admits, pulling off his glasses.

"And did you further know," Sam goes on, "that North Middle School is on a field trip at this zoo right this minute, and they have Anton tied up on their bus?"

"How do you know this?" Mr. Spade asks.

Sam cocks her head. "Well," she says, "I don't."

Mr. Spade slides on his glasses. "Sam," he says.

"Not yet!" she says. "But if I can go check those buses right now, I'm sure I'll find proof!"

Mr. Spade sighs. "Get inside and watch the movie." He points to the doors.

The group trudges inside, Sam fuming the whole way.

THE END

To FOLLOW ANOTHER PATH, TURN TO PAGE 11.

"So," Egg says, "should we keep going?"

"No point in coming in if we stop here," Gum says as he pulls a piece of gum from his pocket. He pops it into his mouth and starts to chew.

"Come on, then," Sam says. She steps forward and knocks the bamboo curtain aside. As she does, the sections of the curtain *click-clack* together in a din like a hundred claves.

From beyond, the birds seem to answer the racket: they caw, they whistle, they screech, and they crow.

The hallway curves out of sight in front of them, forking off in either direction. Only a bit of light is visible on the wall ahead. The bird sounds echo through the bend, bouncing and blending and warping into a deafening and terrifying roar.

"I don't like this," Cat says, grabbing hold of Sam's arm.

"It's just birds," Sam says. "They won't hurt us."

TURN THE PAGE.

"Yeah," Gum says, grinning over his shoulder. "Besides, I thought *birds* were afraid of *cats*, not the other way around." He laughs. "Get it?"

The others roll their eyes.

Gum leads the junior detectives down the left fork. They pass netted windows protecting hawks and eagles on one side, and owls on the other. The owls' enclosure is dark, lit only by pale blue light to mimic moonlight.

A hawk screeches and takes off from its branch as they pass, soaring up into the high net at the top of the enclosure.

Beyond are two doors that lead into the outside section of Bird Land.

"We won't find anything that way," Cat points out. "It's all visible from the zoo paths."

Gum puts his hands on his hips and sighs. "Other fork, then," he says, "I guess."

The four friends turn around and head back toward the darkness of the entrance. Before they take five steps, though, they freeze.

TURN TO PAGE 86.

Now, though the birds have calmed down a bit, the sound of footsteps echoes along the hallways, ringing out of the darkness.

"Uh-oh," Gum says. "We're cornered."

Cat shakes her head. "Come on. To the outdoor section. We can hide there."

But before they reach the doors, a man's voice stops them in their tracks.

"Aha!" he says, angry. "There you four are. I thought I'd find you in here."

Cat, Egg, Sam, and Gum turn around and find Gloria and her father. She's crying. His face is twisted in an angry scowl.

"Let's go," he says. "I think we'll all have a word with Mr. Spade. I have a feeling you four will be spending the rest of this field trip on the bus."

THE END

TO FOLLOW ANOTHER PATH, TURN TO PAGE 11.

"You two should have heard him," Sam says, shaking her head. "He sounded like a real creep."

"And seen him," Gum adds. "He walks like this." Gum hunches his back and drags one foot as he walks across the theater lobby, moaning like a zombie: "Nuuhhhhh . . . Nuhhhhh!"

Cat giggles and covers her mouth.

Egg shakes his head. "You're exaggerating."

"Not even a little!" Gum insists.

Smiling, Sam says to Cat and Egg, "I'm telling you, this guy was straight out of central casting. He's the bad guy."

"Central casting?" Cat says.

"Like for a movie," Egg explains. "He looked like a movie bad guy."

"An *old* movie," Gum adds.

"Speaking of movies," Cat says, taking Sam's hand and pulling her along, "ours is about to start. Let's go!"

TURN THE PAGE.

"But what about . . . you know," Gum says, breaking into his impersonation once more. "Nuhhh . . ."

Egg rolls his eyes. "Come on," he says. "It's *Anton*. He's probably hiding somewhere, causing trouble and loving every minute of it. Now it's movie time."

Gum shrugs. "You're probably right," he says. He turns to Sam. "What do you think?"

Sam smirks. "I guess if you two want to watch the movie," she says to Cat and Egg, "we will watch the movie. But I'm telling you, that guy is a no-goodnik."

"You and your weird words," Cat says, smiling. "Come on, I'll buy us a popcorn."

Before long, the four friends have found seats in the darkening movie theater. It has a huge curved screen that climbs up and over the seats, so it feels like the movie is surrounding them.

The lights fade and then turn off completely, and the screen lights up with the rich greens and blues of a prehistoric landscape.

The ground — and the theater seats — begin to shake with the *boom boom boom* of megafauna footsteps.

"Whoa," Gum says. "This is awesome."

The movie is beautiful and sometimes terrifying. More than once, Cat shrieks and grabs hold of Sam's arm. More than once, Gum leans forward in his seat, mouth wide, and hollers along with some classmates at the saber-toothed cat, the terror bird, and the charging mastodon.

By the time it's over, all four friends — even Sam — are convinced that the age of giant mammals was the most thrilling era of Earth's history.

"I wish I could go back and photograph some of those beasts," Egg says. "I'll have to settle for elephants and giraffes, I guess."

They pass into the lobby with the rest of their class and are greeted by the confusion of shouting voices, a woman crying, and Mr. Spade, his head down and his glasses off, looking very ashamed of himself.

TURN TO PAGE 97.

"Hi, Naomi," Cat says, sidling up to the girl as she walks away from the concession stand, a bag of popcorn in her arm and a large soda in her hand.

"Oh, Catalina," Naomi says as Gum, Egg, and Sam join them. "Um, and all of you. Hi. I take it you're investigating a crime?"

Cat smiles. "You know us too well."

Naomi shrugs. "I'm an observant person," she says, strolling across the lobby. "It's in my nature."

The four friends follow her to a bench, where Naomi sits down. "So, what can I do for you?"

"It's about Anton's disappearance," Egg says, sitting down next to Naomi.

"Of course," Naomi says.

"We hear you're on the math team with him," Sam says, pulling out her notebook and little pencil. "Is that true?"

Naomi nods. "Anton's one of our best," she says. "He's a real ace with quadratic equations and the regular polyhedrons."

"Sure," Gum says. "Me too."

Naomi glances at him and rolls her eyes. "Anyway," she says, "Anton's a troublemaker. I'm sure he's just playing a prank."

"He probably is," Cat says. "I guess you need him to show up soon for the meet today, huh?"

Naomi nods.

"Who are you, um, mathing against?" Gum asks, scratching his head.

"North Middle School," Naomi says. "It would be nice to beat them."

"Rivals?" Egg asks.

"You can say that," Naomi says. She laughs. "Funny. I saw a man earlier — over near Bird Land — and I recognized him, but I couldn't place his face."

"Why is that funny?" Egg asks.

"Because now that you ask about the meet, I remember," Naomi says. "He's the coach of North's math team."

TURN THE PAGE.

The four junior detectives exchange a glance. Sam scribbles in her notepad.

"Well," Naomi says, standing up, "I'd better grab a seat in there. It's getting pretty crowded."

"Oh, we'll be along in a few minutes," Cat says. "Thanks for talking to us."

When Naomi is out of earshot, the four friends huddle up.

"What do you think?" Cat asks.

"It's our best lead," Sam says, closing her notebook and slipping it into her back pocket.

"It's our *only* lead," Egg points out.

"We'd better get a move on," Gum says. "If we wait till after the movie, it might be too late."

"So what do we do?" Cat asks. "If Anton is in trouble at Bird Land, we can't exactly handle it ourselves — not if he's being guarded."

Sam glances over at the theater office, where Mr. Spade is talking to a woman in a security uniform. "Then we'll get some help," she says.

Turn to page 100.

"This seems pretty fishy," Sam says, stroking her chin.

"It sure does," Egg says. He calls to Gloria's dad, "Mr. Wendice, I think we should investigate."

"What for?" Mr. Wendice says.

"Like you said," Gum says, "it's odd. Bird Land isn't closed. What if Anton went in there and got trapped?"

Mr. Wendice says, "Why would he ever go in here?"

Sam shrugs. "Who knows with Anton? It wouldn't hurt to check it out, would it?"

Mr. Wendice thinks for a second and then grabs the door handle. He gives it a yank. It swings open. "Oh!" he says. "I thought it'd be locked. I guess Anton's not trapped in there; not if the door's open."

"True," Cat says, glaring at Sam.

Sam sighs. She says to Mr. Wendice, "The truth is, we think the Closed sign might be a cover for a kidnapper who's got Anton tied up in there."

TURN THE PAGE.

Mr. Wendice's eyebrows go up. "That's some theory," he says. "You'd better let me lead the way."

He ducks under the tape. Gloria hurries after him and grabs his hand. The four junior detectives follow along.

All around them are models of ancient, extinct birds. Their creepy shadows fall across the floor.

Gloria's father moves aside the bamboo curtain that keeps the birds inside the enclosure. The noise of the bamboo knocking against itself rouses the birds. Soon the place is full of caws and screeches.

Cat and Sam jump. Gloria squeezes her dad's hand tighter.

"They're only birds," Mr. Wendice says. "And it's lighter up ahead."

Sam grumbles, "I mean, there was a whole movie about killer birds . . ."

He leads the kids around a curve to the right. The hallway ends in a low room with a domed, clear ceiling. It lets in filtered sunlight, casting the round room in an eerie gloom.

At the far end is a closed glass door, marked with a sign reading

BIRD LAND SHOW
NEXT SHOWING AT 3:30

"No one here," Mr. Wendice says.

"We should check the other side," Sam says, pointing over her shoulder.

"All right," Mr. Wendice says. But Gloria has let go of his hand and walked to the Bird Land Show door. She opens it.

The others hurry to her side. They can just make out the sloping floor and curved seating area of a small auditorium.

"Hello?" Gloria calls down into the darkness. "Anyone in there?"

To everyone's surprise, a voice calls back. "Hello? Is someone there? Help me!"

"Anton!" Cat shouts, and three of the sleuths charge into the room. Egg, for some reason, lags behind, but then catches up to them.

TURN TO PAGE 104.

Sam hurries over to the scene. Standing with Mr. Spade are the principal of Franklin Middle School, three zoo security guards, and a woman with her face in her hands, sobbing.

Cat, Gum, and Egg run up beside Sam.

"I know that woman," Cat whispers. "I think it's Anton's mom."

"Oh, no," Sam says. "This looks serious."

"And another thing, Mr. Spade," the principal says. "Franklin Middle School is not the sort of school that allows teachers to *lose* students on field trips, and we will not have any teachers on staff who let that happen."

"What?" Gum says, stepping into the fray. "You can't be serious."

"Please, kids," Mr. Spade says quietly, gently nudging his two students away. "Not now."

"Not now?" Sam says. "Then when?"

"Yeah!" Cat says. "This is totally unfair!"

"It's an injustice!" Egg adds.

TURN THE PAGE.

"That no-good Anton is probably off spray-painting his name on a bridge someplace," Gum says, facing the principal, "and you're going to *fire* Mr. Spade for it?"

"You should be kicking Anton out of school!" Sam says. She faces Anton's crying mother, who's lifted her head from her hands to watch the argument. "You know your son is a troublemaker who picks on people, right?"

The woman gasps, her hand on her chest. "My Anton would never pick on anyone! And he's not a troublemaker!"

"She didn't mean that, Ms. Gutman," Mr. Spade says, reaching out a hand to comfort Anton's mom.

The woman scowls at him and knocks his hand away. "Don't you touch me!" she says. "I won't rest until you lose your job and your teaching license!"

"Please," Mr. Spade says, using both arms to shuffle the junior detectives away. "Let me handle this. You're just making things worse."

"She's sure upset," Sam says as she sits on a bench along the wall.

Cat sits beside her and drops her chin in her hand. "Maybe Anton really *is* in trouble," she says.

It's nearly time to leave when a pair of security guards strides into the lobby, escorting a boy in a baseball cap between them.

"Anton!" the four friends yell.

"He got lost. But we found him!" says one of the guards. They lead Anton to his mother, who drops to her knees, crying now with joy.

Anton looks at the four friends and smiles a mean smile. Sam sees the outline of a spray-paint can in his pocket. She sighs, nudges Gum, and points to it. All four look at each other.

"No, he would never be a troublemaker," Sam says. The junior detectives all snicker.

THE END

TO FOLLOW ANOTHER PATH, TURN TO PAGE 11.

Sam runs across the lobby with her three best friends following as best they can.

"Mr. Spade!" Sam calls when she's close enough for him to hear.

The teacher looks up from his conversation with the woman from security. Cat's pretty sure she sees him mutter, "Oh, no."

Sam stops in front of him. "We need your help," she says, breathlessly.

"I'm very busy right now, Samantha," Mr. Spade says as Gum, Cat, and Egg arrive.

"I know," Sam says. "Because of Anton. But we know where he is."

Mr. Spade cocks his head. "You do?" he says. Then, more warily, "How?"

"We asked the right questions," Egg says.

The four junior detectives lead the group to Bird Land. Its double doors are blocked with yellow tape, and a sign reads

CLOSED TODAY FOR REPAIRS

The security chief pulls her walkie-talkie from her belt. "Any reason Bird Land should be closed today, maintenance?" she asks.

The device crackles back, "That's a negative, chief. No repairs scheduled at Bird Land today."

"Roger that," the chief says. She holsters her walkie-talkie and with both hands tugs the tape from the doors. She turns to Mr. Spade and his crime-solving students. "You five, wait here," she says. "We don't know what we'll find inside."

She pulls the door open and steps into the darkness of Bird Land's entryway. Her two officers follow along, their batons drawn.

For several minutes, nothing happens.

"Oh, I can't take it," Cat says, bouncing on her toes. "I hope they're OK in there."

"How long do we wait?" Mr. Spade says. "Should we call for backup?"

"It's a delicate operation," Sam says, leaning on Bird Land's exterior wall. "Be patient."

Turn to page 103.

A few seconds later, shouts come from inside the building. Cat grabs Sam's arm.

The doors to Bird Land fly open, and the two security officers, holding a man by both arms, come through.

"That must be the North Middle School math coach," Cat says.

The chief comes out behind her officers, leading Anton.

"I suppose I have to thank you dorks for figuring out where I was," Anton says, standing in front of Sam, Cat, Egg, and Gum.

Gum says. "I just can't believe you're on the math team!"

Anton narrows his eyes. "Don't tell anyone, or else!" he threatens as the chief and Mr. Spade lead him away.

Sam and her friends grin at each other.

THE END

TO FOLLOW ANOTHER PATH, TURN TO PAGE 11.

The kids and their chaperone call out to Anton as they stumble down the steps toward the stage.

"Where are you?" Sam yells as she steps onto the stage.

"I'm backstage!" Anton shouts. "Get me out of here!"

Sam and Mr. Wendice — with his cell phone's flashlight on — weave between wooden backdrops painted to look like snowy peaks, dark pine forests, and wild, rainy jungles. Beyond, they find a heavy black door and pull it open.

"He's here!" Mr. Wendice shouts, running forward.

In the middle of the small backstage room, Anton is crouched inside a cage, his hands on the bars, eyes wide and scared. "Let me out!"

"We're here, Anton," Mr. Wendice says, kneeling beside the cage. Sam hurries to his side, and together they figure out how to remove the locking pin and free Anton.

Anton falls into Mr. Wendice's arms.

"Are you OK?" Cat says as she reaches backstage.

"I think so," Anton says.

"Who did this to you?" Gum asks.

Anton shakes his head. "I don't know," he says. "I just followed a trail of mini candy bars into the bird house. Next thing I knew, I was in a cage!"

"Anton," Cat says, crossing her arms. "Don't you know not to eat candy you find on the ground?"

"I wasn't going to eat it," Anton says. "I was going to *sell* it to kids in the class."

"We can talk about everything that's wrong with that later," Egg says. "For now, let's get out of here before the kidnapper comes back!"

"That is a spectacular idea," Mr. Wendice says. The sleuths, Anton, and Mr. Wendice hurry through the door into the auditorium. Just at that moment, the house lights go on.

TURN THE PAGE.

"Not so fast!" says a man's voice.

"Coach Ellison?" Mr. Wendice says, looking up at the darkened doorway. "Is that you?"

The man says in a deeper voice, "What? From North Middle School? Don't be ridiculous."

"It *is* you," Mr. Wendice says.

"Of course it is," says Sam. "He knows that if Anton is gone, the Franklin Middle School team will have to forfeit."

"That's ridiculous!" says the voice. But the door slams shut and the lock clicks. Everyone rushes up the stairs and Mr. Wendice tries the handle of the door, but they're too late.

"Now what?" Cat asks.

"I have no cell service in here," Mr. Wendice adds, looking at his phone.

"Not to worry," Egg says, dropping into a seat.

"How can you say that?" Anton says.

"Just wait," Egg says, and a moment later the door flies open again. Coach Ellison steps in — trailed by the zoo's security chief, two officers, and Mr. Spade.

"How did you do that?" Sam asks.

"Simple," Egg says. "I called zoo security before we came in here!"

THE END

TO FOLLOW ANOTHER PATH, TURN TO PAGE 11.

literary news

MYSTERIOUS WRITER REVEALED!

Steve Brezenoff is the author of the Field Trip Mysteries, the Museum Mysteries, and the Ravens Pass series of thrillers, as well as three novels for older readers. Steve lives in Minneapolis, Minnesota, with his wife, Beth, and their two children, Sam and Etta.

arts & entertainment

ARTIST IS KEY TO SOLVING MYSTERY, SAY POLICE

Marcos Calo lives happily in A Coruña, Spain, with his wife, Patricia (who is also an illustrator), and their daughter, Claudia. When Marcos and Patricia aren't drawing, they like to go on long walks by the sea. They also watch a lot of films and eat Nutella™ sandwiches. Yum!

A Detective's Dictionary

animatronic — a lifelike puppet that is animated by a mechanical device

claves — hardwood sticks that a player hits together to make sound

forfeit — to give something up

megafauna — large animals

narrate — to tell a story or recall events

no-goodnik — someone who is a troublemaker

ruse — a plan to fool or trick someone

scoundrel — a person who likes to trick people or is mean to others

sidling — the act of moving next to someone quietly

snicker — a short laugh, sometimes disrespectful

snookums — a term of endearment: a pet name

FURTHER INVESTIGATIONS

CASE #YCSFTMTMBS17

1. Many of the kids and teachers think Anton is playing a prank. Discuss what reasons they give in the story. Do you think they should have been more worried?

2. Gloria seems scared of many things in the zoo. Have you ever been scared on a trip? Talk about how you felt and why you were scared.

3. Why do you think the Field Trip Mysteries gang likes to solve mysteries? Do you like to solve mysteries? Have there been any mysteries in your life that you have solved successfully?

IN YOUR OWN DETECTIVE'S NOTEBOOK . . .

1. Ms. Halliday was very sad and upset that her hardware store would have competition from a much bigger store. Write a letter from Ms. Halliday to the CEO of the big hardware store asking him or her not to build across the street from Ms. Halliday's store. Make sure to list reasons why.

2. Mr. Spade often gets frustrated with the Field Trip Mysteries gang for not following directions. Write a letter from Sam to Mr. Spade explaining why the gang seems to go its own way when it comes to solving mysteries.

3. The Field Trip Mysteries gang is surprised when they find out Anton is on the math team. Write down five reasons why assuming things about people might not be a good idea.

WAIT!
DON'T close the book!
There's
MORE!
FIND MORE:
games
puzzles
heroes
villains
authors
illustrators at...
www.
capstonekids
.com
Still want MORE?
Find cool websites and more books like this one at www.Facthound.com.
Just type in the Book ID: 9781496526427 and you're ready to go!